Which Animal Are You?

Who decided on the name for the horse with
the hump and the hooves and the
nothing-much-of-a-tail?

What became of the Highly Active Mighty
Small Toothy Eary Rat?

Why was the largest, fattest ant of all quite so
terrifying?

Anthony Smith's delightful stories describing
how the animals got their names were first told
on BBC TV's *Jackanory*.

WHICH ANIMAL ARE YOU?

ANTHONY SMITH

As told on Jackanory

Illustrated by

Jan Brychta

BBC BOOKS

For Zena

Published by BBC Books
A division of BBC Enterprises Ltd
Woodlands, 80 Wood Lane, London W12 0TT

First published 1988
©Anthony Smith 1988

ISBN 0 563 20637 3

Typeset in Great Britain by Wilmaset, Birkenhead
Bound by Richard Clay Ltd, Bungay, Suffolk

Contents

ONE   I Came Last   9

TWO   The Ha-ma-sa-ta-e-ras   27

THREE   Norib and Ibron   45

FOUR   The Biggest Cats   63

FIVE   The L. F. Ant   81

ONE
I Came Last

One day a few of the animals thought it would be fun to have a race. Of course, quite a few more thought that a race was the last thing they wanted.

"It strikes me as being particularly silly," said the tortoise. "You spend all your time rushing past places and never stop to have a decent look at *any* of them."

"I always like where I am," said the sloth. "I keep on finding another leaf I haven't properly investigated, and what's the point of rushing on?"

So the sloth stayed absolutely where he was, quite content with the world around him. He too

could never see the point of rushing past places. Indeed he always looked as if he could never see the point of anything.

"Oh, come on," said the horse, "a race would be terrific."

And he suddenly galloped off to do a little practice run, which proved to be much further than the tortoise had ever been in his entire life. It was even further than the sloth had ever heard about. Poor sloth! As he couldn't see the point in a race, he could see even less point in running about before the race began.

"Oh, come on," said the horse again, when he had come back, not even puffed and not even thinking he had been anywhere, "we do all need a race."

"I'll join you," said the cheetah.

Now cheetahs always think they can win races, mainly because they are the very fastest animals. That seems a good enough reason for winning, but what the cheetahs forget is that they never go very far. So they do win to begin with, but then they stop to tell everyone they've won.

"You haven't done anything of the sort," say the horses to the cheetahs as they gallop past. But the cheetahs think they have won and think it is silly of the horses to go on running after the race is over.

The trouble with all these races was that the same things happened every time. A horse would suggest the idea and the same animals, such as the zebras, the gazelles and the antelopes – or rather, lots and lots of different sorts of antelope – would

join in. The sloth and the tortoise weren't the only animals who refused to race. The mole and the squirrel never joined in either. The mole would have been happy to join, provided that the race was underground. And the squirrel would also have been happy to join, provided no one was allowed to touch the ground but just rushed through the trees. As the horses never liked these ideas, and the cheetahs didn't, and the zebras didn't, and the gazelles didn't, and not a single antelope liked them, the races were always run along the surface. And always the cheetahs said they had won, and always the horses told them they hadn't. But no one ever knew who actually had won, particularly as there was no winning post. Perhaps that is why the horses kept on suggesting a race. They not only liked the idea of running, but also wanted to know who would win.

This particular race looked like being just the same as all the others. The mole said he couldn't see any point in it and disappeared from sight. The squirrel also said it would be a dull race, without a single branch to run along, and he

vanished up his favourite tree. The sloth and the tortoise didn't bother to vanish. They stayed where they were, not thinking about anything much, but knowing that races were stupid. They had each found a leaf to chew and knew they wouldn't have found those leaves if they had been racing. They might have found other leaves but, as they always said, what's wrong with the nearest leaf? It tastes as good as any other.

Anyway, the same old starters all lined up in the same old fashion. The horse kicked at the ground, impatient to get going. The cheetah idled about, knowing he could catch them up. And all the antelopes and gazelles and zebras stood in a line by the horse, just as they always did. The elephant was always the one to start them off because he could make such a terrific trumpeting noise. So, in this latest race, everyone was lined up, and the elephant lifted his trunk, and even the cheetah began to think it was time to stop idling about, when suddenly there was a noise like someone being sick.

"Urrgghhh," came the noise again, and everyone wondered who was making it.

Some animals thought it was the elephant, who often made very funny noises with his stomach, but no one dared say so and it wasn't him anyway. Lots of animals knew it couldn't possibly have been them because they were *never* sick; and lots more animals knew it hadn't been them, because if you've just been sick, you *know* you've been sick, don't you? The sloth didn't know, because it took him such a long time to know anything; but, in any case, he wouldn't have been sick quite so quickly.

"Urrgghhh," came the noise yet again, to remind everybody how nasty it was. It was quite unlike any other animal noise – except of course for the elephant's stomach rumbles, which no one dared to mention.

Then someone noticed a brand-new kind of animal coming towards them from the direction of the desert. He was rather like a horse, but he did have this hump in the middle of his back. His legs were long like a horse's legs, but each ended in two hooves instead of one. And he had a tail, which a horse also has, but it was a pathetic nothing of a tail, more like a bit of old rope that happened to be hanging there. The most important difference of all was that he made this 'urrgghhh' noise, which no horse could ever make even if it tried.

"What on earth are you?" asked the animals.

"Urrgghhh," said the newcomer, as if that was answer enough, which, in a way, it was.

The new animal just stood there, with his hump, his cloven hooves, his dusty, sandy colour, looking as if he might make that terrible noise all over again. As it was a bit rude staring at the newcomer, and as they were about to have their race, someone said:

"We're going to have a race. Would you like to take part?"

"That would be very nice," he said, proving that he didn't just say 'urrgghhh'. "But where are we racing to, and for how many weeks?"

"Weeks!" said the cheetah. "More like seconds!"

"It'll take longer than that," said the horse. "In fact, it will be a longish race."

"In that case," said the newcomer, "I'll go and get ready." And he disappeared from sight.

This was too much for the elephant, who still had his trunk up and was wanting to give the starting trumpet noise. So, without any more ado, he gave it, and everyone was deafened for it was VERY LOUD. Anyway, even the cheetah stopped idling about and they all started running.

All except our newcomer, with the hump, the cloven hooves and the nothing-much-of-a-tail. He was busy preparing. If it was to be a longish race, he thought he had better fill up with water. So he found a little pool and drank it all up. Then he

thought some food would be in order. So he found some thorny, prickly, dry-as-dust bushes that no one else would eat, and he gobbled them all up, every last thorn and every last prickle. Then he hurried back to the starting line for the race.

"They've all gone," said the elephant. "They all went yesterday. What on earth have you been doing?"

"Oh, just getting ready," said the newcomer.

"Well, you'd better hurry off after them," said the elephant, "and don't waste any more time."

And that is what the newcomer did. With a final "urrgghhh" he walked up to the elephant, and then ran off in the direction the others had taken. He had a funny kind of run because both his left legs worked more or less at the same time, and then both his right legs. This made him wobble from side to side.

"He can't possibly win," said the elephant. "I thought that before he started, but now that I've seen him run I'm even more convinced. No one should run like that. At least no one who wants to win a race."

The newcomer had only run for about five

minutes when he came across the cheetah lying flat on an ant heap.

"It's all over," said the cheetah. "I won easily. In fact I won yesterday, and I don't know what you're doing still running."

"I'm not *still* running," said the humpy, two-hooved, rope-tailed newcomer, all full of water and prickly spikes. "I've only just begun to run. In any case, what's wrong with being second?"

So he ran on, and the cheetah laughed so much at the sight that he fell right off his ant heap. By the time he had picked himself up, the newcomer was almost out of sight, waddle, waddle, left, left, right, right. The cheetah laughed again, but held on tighter this time. Then he yawned and went to sleep. It was exhausting, winning races.

Meanwhile the newcomer hurried on, waddle, waddle, left, left, right, right. With all those prickles and all that water inside him, he knew he could keep going for a very long time. What he didn't know was that everyone else, and not just the cheetah, had now dropped out of the race. The horse had seen a hedgerow, full of lots of grass and tasty-looking flowers. All of a sudden he felt that he had had enough of running and nothing like enough of eating. So he stopped and ate some grass, and then ate some flowers, and then ate some more of both. Finally he was full, and he couldn't even be bothered to lie down.

All the other competitors had also seen something to their fancy and forgotten about the running. The gazelles saw some dry-looking plants and thought they just had to be nibbled. Some of the antelopes stopped by a swamp, full of tall, delicious-looking reeds, and others stopped by a wood, full of young trees asking to be eaten. So the race had petered out. They always did, with no one quite sure who had won. Of course the cheetah knew, but no one believed him. They all felt he was, well, a bit of a cheat, and that was how he got his name. You can't just run for five minutes, and then stop. That's, well, cheating, and only a cheater would do that!

But the newcomer didn't know any of this. He had seen the swamp and the wood. He had seen the reeds and the young trees, but he hadn't seen anyone eating them. In any case he was mainly looking ahead, wondering if he could catch up the others – wherever they were. He had a terrible feeling that he was going to be last, and that made him a bit sad. He knew he wasn't the greatest runner in the world, but he still didn't want to be last. So he ran and ran, waddled and waddled for days and days and days.

After two weeks he felt a little thirsty. The pool of water he had drunk had been a long time ago. All those nice prickly leaves and spiky twigs were now only a distant memory, and he thought how nice it would be to find and eat some more. But what he wanted to find even more was one animal ahead of him. If he could overtake one animal, just one, he wouldn't be quite last. Being one from last would, he felt, be very much better. Of course, he didn't know there was absolutely no one in front of him, but he kept on running and running, waddling and waddling, getting thirstier and hungrier, until suddenly he could run no more. For a time he just stood there, getting his breath, and then he thought he had better mark the place that he had reached. But he was so ashamed of himself for coming last he could think of nothing else to write in the sand except "I came last". He was very, very sad about it, and he stamped out the letters with his big cloven hooves, plain for all to see.

I CAME LAST

Then he walked away, to look for a bunch of prickly spikes and some water to wash them down. A lovely shower of rain then poured down – just what he wanted. But it washed at the letters he had written, and first washed away the I. Then, at the other end, it washed away the A and

the S and the T. So there was nothing left except
'CAME L'. Some gazelles were the first to read
it. They saw the footprints. They knew who had
made them. And they read Came l. "So that's who
it was," they said. From that moment on they
knew the name of the humpy, sandy-coloured
creature who said 'urrgghhh' from time to time
and had a tail more like a rope than any decent
tail. And now you all know how the camel got his
name.

TWO
The Ha-ma-sa-ta-e-ras

Poor old Noah did have a terrible time. First of all he had to build the ark, and he had never built such a thing before. Then he had to make sure all the animals got on board. Not only did there have to be room for them, but he had to make sure he had lots of the right kind of food. It was no good expecting a lion to eat grass, and an anteater just wouldn't be happy with a ham sandwich. Finally, and worst of all, he had to know who everybody was. He had to know whether there were two of them already in the ark. There wouldn't be room for any extras, so he had to know who had already

arrived. In other words, they all had to have names.

This was even more important after they had got on board. After all, they were going to be there for forty days and forty nights, and they all had to be organised, fed, given water and kept comfortable during that time. It was no good Noah saying to someone, "Could you feed the animals next to those animals you fed yesterday which were near the ones you gave water to and below the others you forgot to give water to." That kind of remark would be muddling even on the first day, let alone on the thirty-ninth. It would always be difficult. "Do you remember those animals who didn't get their hay and made a

big fuss which woke up those other animals who had got too much hay; well, could you make certain they're all right now, and on the way give water to those animals who drink so much, and make certain the others next to them are not fighting . . ." It would be a nightmare, a forty-nightmare, and a forty-daymare as well, if there is such a thing.

Noah didn't know the names of all the animals, for who could possibly know that? After all, there are more than 8000 different kinds of bird in the world, and then there are all the four-legged animals, such as lions and tigers, and rats and mice, and then there are the no-legged animals, like snakes and worms, and eight-legged animals like spiders, and hundred-legged animals like centipedes. It must all have been terribly muddling, particularly for a man who had only just built a boat in record time. Even fifty is a lot of names to remember (do you know the names of fifty animals?), and Noah had thousands in his ark, in fact tens of thousands, in fact hundreds of thousands. So think of poor Noah trying to remember all those names. And think of him trying to do so for forty days and forty nights.

Well, after about one day and one night, he knew he would never be able to remember them all. No sooner had he learnt a new name than he forgot one he had already learned. So he thought it might be better if he gave them numbers. Of course, he didn't have to give numbers to the animals he already knew a lot about. He knew about things like cats and dogs – after all it had been raining cats and dogs – and cows and sheep and pigs and chickens. And, like most people, he knew about lions and tigers, elephants and zebras, and all sorts of others. But there were thousands more he had never even heard of, let alone seen – strange creatures such as ruffed lemurs, pig-tailed macaques and lesser-spotted woodpeckers. "Yes, that's who we are," said the ruffed lemurs, pig-tailed macaques and lesser-spotted woodpeckers.

But as they all came on board together and all spoke at the same time, Noah knew he would forget their names at once. And so he did.

"I think they were the pig-spotted peckers, or was it the rough-tailed wood-caques? Oh dear, I shall never know," he said, and he never did.

Worst of all were the hundreds and hundreds of small furry animals. They were a bit like mice, but sometimes more like voles, and their ears were big or small, and their tails short or long, and their fur short or furry, and they all scampered about, and squeaked a lot, and said they were different from each other. Noah couldn't take them seriously and gave them numbers at once. So there was mouse-1 and mouse-2 and mouse-3-yellow-tooth, and even mouse-4-yellow-tooth-squeaker, and Noah longed for the rain to end. A lot of these furry, toothy, squeaking, perhaps-with-a-tail, perhaps-not, animals didn't do anything for the whole voyage except curl up in a ball inside a bit of hay. And they were certainly the last to leave the ark.

In time Noah started inventing different kinds of names. These were not so much what the animals seemed to be, but what they seemed to have done to him. He called one Head-Bang because he happened to hit his head one day when he was feeding it. So there was Foot-Stub, Knee-

Knock, Shoulder-Bruise, Ankle-Twist, Finger-Pinch-1 and Finger-Pinch-2, and Stop-making-that-terrible-noise, because that's what Noah said every time he passed it.

Even the animals didn't know each other's names – mainly because they had never met before. How could the kookaburra know about the condor when they both lived in different parts of the world? And even the Malayan tapir didn't know about the Brazilian tapir until they saw each other going on board. Then they were absolutely delighted to see someone else looking as handsome and rugged and interesting as they were.

"You're quite the most exciting animal I have ever seen," said the Brazilian tapir to the Malayan tapir.

"You took the words right out of my mouth," said the Malayan tapir to the Brazilian tapir before they hurried inside, laughing happily.

Noah called them Boring 1 and Boring 2, and that stopped both pairs of tapirs from laughing at once. In fact, to the best of everyone's knowledge, no one has ever seen any kind of tapir laughing from that day to this.

During the forty days and forty nights, apart from thinking about food and when they might be allowed out of the ark, many of the animals also thought about names for the very first time in their lives. They hadn't realised how important names were.

"Hey you, whoever you are, come here and meet whoever my friend is, and then we can join whoever that is over there," they would shout to each other.

This was confusing for everyone. It also wasted a lot of time and was rather rude.

"I'd never thought much about names before I got on the ark," said the worm. No one thought the worm had ever thought about anything, but they had to agree with him.

"Even I," said the owl, "even I, who am supposed to think of everything, hadn't given the subject much thought. I must now think why I hadn't thought about it before." And he closed both his eyes in order to think why he hadn't ever thought before of what he should have thought of.

On the day that they left the ark the animals didn't immediately rush off to the bits of the Earth where they should live. They chatted with the friends they had met on board, and continued their talk about names.

"I think a name should be short, different from all the others, and easy to spell," said the warthog. "For example, 'warthog' is a good name."

"What's wrong with a name being even shorter?" said the owl.

"I can't spell 'owl'," said the warthog.

"Not everyone can have a short name," said the duck-billed platypus. "There just aren't enough short names to go round."

"I agree," said the double-wattled cassowary.

"This is ridiculous," said the warthog. "What you both have aren't so much names as descriptions. It's as if I was to call myself toothy-tusky, ugly-mugly."

"That's a good name," said the duck-billed platypus.

"I agree," said the double-wattled cassowary, who never did seem to say anything else. Just because he was a big bird didn't mean that he had a big brain.

"Quite ridiculous," said the warthog with a sneer, giving everyone a good look at his teeth and making them shut up. He was fierce at times, and you had to pretend you thought he was right even when he might be wrong. The double-wattled cassowary had been about to say that he thought toothy-tusky, ugly-mugly was a wonderful name, but he remembered those teeth, and said "I agree" instead.

At that moment someone noticed another pair of small, furry animals coming down the plank from the ark, looking as if they had overslept. This pair had spent the entire voyage curled up in the hay. No one had even seen them, let alone met them or learnt their names. The warthog went up to speak to them.

"Hello," he said, "and who are you?"

"Well, we're us, aren't we?" they said, both nodding their heads at each other.

"I mean, what's your name?" said the warthog.

"How should we know?" they said. "Isn't a name something that other people use? We call each other 'us' and this is 'me'."

As they were both speaking at once, this made everything harder for the warthog. It was harder still for the double-wattled cassowary, who wanted to agree but didn't quite know what to agree with.

"So, what do you call us?" asked the two small furry creatures, the very last to come out of the ark.

"I don't know," said the warthog.

"None of us know," said the owl, hating the thought that one of the others might know something he didn't. "But we'd all like to know."

"I agree," said the double-wattled cassowary, who had been longing to speak, and had at last got something to agree about.

"You have to have a name," said the crocodile, who had been silent until then. He was very keen on names, and got terribly cross when anyone called him alligator by mistake.

"Then you'll have to give us one," said the furry pair, who felt a bit frightened at seeing the crocodile quite so close.

"We can't just invent a name," said the warthog. "I've been called warthog for as long as I can remember."

"That's a long, long time," said the wild boar, who never missed an opportunity for getting at the warthog. "I suggest we call them Highly Active, because they haven't stopped fidgeting since we've been talking to them."

"Are they so active?" asked the elephant. "I can't see from up here, but they are Mighty Small."

"Let's call them Highly Active Mighty Small," said the duck-billed platypus. "I like long names."

"That's a silly name," said the crocodile. "Let's call them Toothy, because they have large ones at the front and teeth *are* very important."

"So are ears," said the elephant. "We might as well call them Eary."

"It's getting better and better," said the duck-billed platypus. "Highly Active Mighty Small Toothy Eary – now that's a terrific name."

"I agree," said the double-wattled cassowary.

"Quite, quite ridiculous," said the warthog. "You can't call anyone that, even if they *are* all of that. I think they're rats. They look rattish to me."

"But that name's already booked," said the owl, who did like to make sure people got things right. "We can't forget the rats can we?" And he laughed as much as an owl can laugh, because he was looking forward very much to eating one.

"Well, rats are just rats and nothing else," said the duck-billed platypus; "but these could be called Highly Active Mighty Small Toothy Eary Rats!"

"Quite, quite, quite ridiculous," said the warthog. "It's far too long, even if you try and speed it up a bit."

"HighlActivMightSmalToothEarRat," said the wild boar, trying both to speed it up a bit *and* get back at the warthog for being so stuffy.

"Huh-Ah-Muh-Suh-Tuh-Er-Ruh," said the

owl, who always did have a different way of saying things, and made it sound more like spelling.

"Ha-A-Ma-Sa-Ta-E-Ra," said the owl once more, trying to make it faster still. Everyone agreed this did sound a bit more like a name, and so the owl tried again.

"Ha-ma-sa-ta-e-ra," said the owl, tremendously fast.

"Ha-mst-er," said everyone else, trying to make it faster still.

"I've got it!" said the warthog. "Hamster – now *that's* a proper name."

"So *that's* who we are," said the two hamsters. "It's good to know."

"It's only quite a good name," said the duck-billed platypus.

"I agree," said the double-wattled cassowary.

"It's got seven letters," said the warthog, "just the right number for a really good name."

"Don't be silly," said the owl. "What better name could there possibly be than owl?"

"What about hamster?" said the hamsters. "It's easy to say and quite easy to spell. In fact, it's much easier to spell than owl."

"Oh, how I agree," said the double-wattled cassowary who, if the truth be known, couldn't spell a single name.

At that moment the animals began to go their separate ways. Some of them had a very long walk ahead of them, and didn't want to waste any more time. But fastest to leave were a group of animals who had been listening to the talk about spelling and who didn't want anyone to ask them how their names were spelt. The truth is they didn't know themselves, and fastest of all was the pair of angwantibo. Then there were the lechwe, the kodkods, the cuscus, the binturong, the tucotuco

and the aye-aye. And if you're wondering why you haven't seen any of these animals it's because they're still afraid that someone might ask them how they spell their names.

But you *do* see hamsters, and their name *is* quite easy to spell – particularly if you remember that they're no more, and certainly no less, than Highly Active Mighty Small Toothy Eary Rats.

THREE
Norib and Ibron

Down on Blackberry Farm there was one bird that was always very curious. It had to see what the other animals were doing, what the gardeners were doing, what everyone was doing. The ducks were never curious – except about mud and whether there was something they hadn't yet seen at the bottom of the pond. The blackbirds weren't curious, except about worms and what might lie under the next leaf they turned over. But the curious bird with the bright red chest was curious about everything. And everyone. And whatever was going on. He didn't know his name, but he

did know practically everything else, such as what happened every day down on the farm. And who said what to whom, and when. He was always inquisitive about all the goings-on, even if they

didn't change very much from day to day.

In particular the food on Blackberry Farm didn't change. Sunday food was just like any other day – nothing special was served up. On every day of every week it was served at the same time, in the same way, in the same buckets, and from the same people.

"Here you are, dog," said Mrs Stevenson, the farmer's wife, putting his food in a bowl.

"Here you are, cat," she said, putting her food on a plate.

"Here you are, pig," said Mr Stevenson, the farmer, pouring his food into a trough.

"Here you are, cow," he said, throwing some hay on the ground.

And then it was the turn of the horse, and the sheep, and the ox. It was always the same. Always the dog finished off the cat's food, and always the dog then sniffed at the pig's food and decided he didn't like it.

"Do you realise," asked the dog, "that all of us who live on Blackberry Farm have got short little names? There's me, dog, and then there's cat, and pig, and cow, and ox, and sheep, and goat, and horse, and no one has a longish name like, well, blackberry."

"Or like Stevenson," said the cat.

"True," said the dog. "Very, very true. Apart from all of us," he added, "there are all the wild creatures, such as rat, and mouse, and mole."

"And worm," said the hen, who liked worms.

"And ant," said the cock, who liked ants.

"Perhaps," said the cat, "perhaps we've got short names because there are lots and lots of us, and if we were a bit rarer we'd have longer names. Let's think of a rare animal and see if it has a long name." But no one could think of a rare animal, even though they thought and thought. It's difficult because it's like trying to remember the name of someone you haven't seen for years and years.

"I know a rare animal," said the owl, who'd been asleep until that moment. "And it's called tyrannosaurus rex."

"That is rare," said everyone else. "It's so rare that we haven't even heard of it."

"It's so rare," added the owl with a sort of smirk, "that you won't ever be able to see it because it's extinct."

"Gosh, that *is* rare," they all said.

"I think," said the dog, "we're getting away from the point, which is that we've got short names because the farmer is always short of time, and he couldn't possibly call us a hairy-nosed wombat even if we were one."

"But no one here is a hairy-nosed wambot," said the cat who always got things wrong.

The dog was about to say 'wombat' but then couldn't be bothered. He thought of chasing the cat, but then decided not to as he often ended such chases with a nasty scratch on his nose.

"Silly old nairy-hosed wambot," said the cat, and got nearer than ever to being chased.

"I would like my name to be longer," said the mouse, who didn't often speak when the cat was around. "For instance, I've often thought I'd like to be called 'Enor-mouse' or even 'Fa-mouse', or perhaps . . ." but he was stopped by the owl.

"You don't spell 'famous' like that," said the owl who could be very annoying at times. "Besides, it's 'fa-muss' and not 'fa-mouse'."

"What's a 'muss'?" said the mouse.

"There's no such thing as a 'muss'," said the owl; "there's only 'fa-muss', which means every-one knows about you."

"Oh dear, we're getting off the point again," said the dog. "At least shorter names are easier to spell than longer ones," he continued. "Even our friend the mouse can spell 'dog'."

"Ah," said the cat, who could be very nasty at times, "but can our friend the mouse spell 'mouse'?"

"Course I can," said the mouse.

"Go on then," said the cat.

"Well," said the mouse, "it starts with an M, a *mer*."

"*Merrhh*," said the cow because that was the only sound she could ever make, and she was delighted to hear the mouse almost make it.

"And after the M comes what?" asked the dog.

"Well, there's an M," said the mouse, "and then there's an O, and then there's a W, and then . . ." but a lot of the animals then started laughing.

53

The cow wasn't laughing because she knew that C O W S spelt cows, and so M O W S should spell mouse. The ox also wasn't laughing because he couldn't spell anything.

"So, who can spell their name?" asked the owl. "Can you, cat?"

"Of course I can," said the cat, letting her claws come out and giving the owl a nasty kind of look.

"Oh, well, perhaps you can," said the owl. "What about you, horse?"

"Course," said the horse. But no one believed him because no one else was very certain how to spell 'horse', particularly after he had said 'course'. That made it very much worse. Come to think of it, how was 'worse' spelt?

"I know what you're all thinking," said the owl, still being annoying. It is annoying to be told that someone else knows what you're thinking, as thoughts are supposed to be private. But the owl was right, annoyingly right.

"Horse is not spelt like 'course'," he said, "or even like a cat's 'paws'. It's spelt like 'worse'." The other animals didn't believe him and started to mutter angrily to each other. The cow was particularly cross.

"You mean to say that 'cows' are not like 'mouse', and 'horse' is not like 'course' but is like 'worse'? This is ridiculous."

"I expect 'ridiculous' is spelt like 'garden gate'," said the mouse, who did like a joke or two from time to time.

"I've been thinking," said the owl, with a glare at the mouse, "that we really ought to settle this spelling business. Let's find out once and for all who can spell their name and who can't."

"How?" said the cow.

"What we've got to do," said the owl, "is to borrow those spelling bricks the children use in the house. They have a different letter on each side, and we can all choose the letters we need to spell our own names."

"Sounds very difficult to me," said the ox, wrinkling his brow at the thought.

"Let's go and get the letters," said the owl, longing for this chance to show that he knew most about everything.

The little bird with the bright red chest had been hopping about like anything while this was going on. The talk of names excited him, particularly as he didn't know what he was called. So he followed the animals up to the house and watched them borrow the bricks. First the mouse went in

to find out where they were. Then the cat, on tiptoe, took them one by one. Finally the pig and cow and sheep and goat and horse all kicked them down to the tractor shed. The ox tried to kick them, but kept on missing and seemed to kick everything else lying in the way, such as old tin

cans. So everyone told him not to help. He looked a bit sad, and added another wrinkle or two to his brow, but the job did get finished much more quickly without him.

The owl hadn't helped at all, but was all ready to give instructions once the bricks had arrived.

"Pick out the letters that spell your name," he said. He swooped down, took an O, a W and an L, and looked terribly smug. No one else had known how to spell owl, but everyone knew he must be right. That smugness said it all. Anyway, the cat saw a K and put out a paw for it. The owl smiled to himself. The mouse took an M and an O and then looked around to see how the others were getting on. The horse took an H but couldn't decide what came next. The ox took nothing as he didn't know even his first letter.

"Here, I'll help you," said the owl, who wasn't usually quite so friendly. He picked out an O and an X and put them in front of the huge animal. The ox pushed them around with his feet and decided upon the correct order. 'XO,' he spelt, and the owl laughed most irritatingly. But so did all the others. It was so nice when someone else got into trouble.

At that moment the little bird with the red chest perched himself on a farm rake and joined in the conversation.

"Hello," he chirruped.

"Hello," said all the others. Everyone knew this bird but, as he always kept himself to himself, no one had ever bothered to ask his name. The pig and the sheep and the goat and the horse and the cow and the cat and the dog and the mouse and the ox all suddenly realised they didn't know it. The owl knew it, of course, and also knew – because he knew everything – that they didn't know it.

"I'll tell you what I'll do," he said. "I'll pick out this bird's letters and then you can all guess what his name is." So he walked over and picked them out in the wrong order – he wasn't going to make it too easy. He then put down an I, a B, an R, an O and an N.

"I know," said the cow at once. "This little bird is an Ibron."

"No, it isn't," said the mouse, who'd been pushing the letters around a bit. "It's a Norib."

"It's a Nibor," said the goat, who liked nibbling at things.

"It's a Brion," said the sheep, who knew he liked eating the plant called bryony.

"You're wrong," said the ox, "it's a Broin."

"I wish *you* had a bit more broin," said the owl, and had a long laugh at his own joke. "Come on," he added, "use your broins, all of you. If it isn't an Ibron, a Norib, a Nibor, a Brion, or a Broin, what is it?"

"I'm so glad it's not," thought the little bird. "I wouldn't like any of that lot for a name. But what am I called?"

Suddenly it was feeding time.

"Here you are, dog; here you are, cat; here you are, pig . . ." came the same old shouts, as Mr and Mrs Stevenson brought out the animals' buckets.

There was a mad rush for the food and the pig ran right through the letters, rearranging them yet again.

The little bird with the bright red chest perched on the first one. It was an R. The next was an O. Then there was a B. And then an I. And then an N.

"Oh dear," he said, "now all the animals have gone, and I shall never know my name. But maybe I'll learn it if I fly near gardeners and listen carefully. I just might hear them say it, if they see me watching them. I do hope I will one day."

FOUR
The Biggest Cats

"I've got something to ask you," said the first Big Cat to the second one day.

"That's funny," said the second Big Cat to the first. "I've got something to ask you."

"Well," said the first one, "I must ask you my question first because I was the first to say I had a question."

"That's only because I let you ask first," said the second one, "but in fact I've had this question at the back of my mind for days, and so I must ask you first."

Very soon there was a fight, with lots of earth-coloured fur flying about, and lots of black and yellow fur to keep it company, and lots of snarling and growling and scratching.

Just at that moment an elephant wandered by. Now nobody argues with an elephant, but elephants are always very interested in other people's arguments.

"What's this all about?" asked the elephant.

"Well, I've got something to say," said the first Big Cat.

"So have I," said the second Big Cat, "and we both want to be first."

"Well, then," said the elephant, "why don't you both speak at once and then you can both be first."

It was so easy being an elephant. An elephant always has the answers to all sorts of problems.

"Right, both of you start speaking when I say so. SO," said the elephant very loudly, half-trumpeting at his own joke.

It took the Big Cats a little time to see what he
meant, but then they both remembered what their
questions were.

"How did the cat get its name?" they both said
together, before adding to each other: "but how
did you know what I was going to say?"

"This is getting difficult," said the elephant.
"You're beginning to sound like an echo."

"No, we're not," they both said, sounding like
an echo.

66

"One at a time," said the elephant, who was beginning to get a bit cross.

"All right, you speak," said the first Big Cat to the second.

"No, you speak," said the second to the first.

Now the elephant did become angry. He threw a lot of dust in the air, made a fearful trumpeting sound, and looked as if he was going to tread on both of them. Eventually he quietened down and even spoke calmly.

"The trouble with being me," he said, "is that I not only know the answers to most questions but sometimes I even know what the questions are before anyone asks me. You want to know how the cat got its name, because you often get called 'Big Cats'. Am I right?"

"Absolutely right," said the Big Cats both together. For a moment the elephant looked cross again, but he also enjoyed being right and he ended up looking rather pleased with himself.

"Yes, I do happen to know the answer to this one," admitted the elephant, smirking more than a little.

"Well, tell us," said the echo.

"Oh, all right," said the elephant. "It is all to do with the birds. There's nothing that birds hate so much as a cat. There they are, all feeding happily, when suddenly a cat lands right in the middle of them. There's hardly time for them to do anything, except open up their wings and fly to safety. But sometimes they do have a little more time to spare and can say 'It's a cat'."

At that point the elephant suddenly stopped in his story.

"You can't end there," said the two Big Cats together all over again. "How do they know it's a cat?"

"Oh, yes," said the elephant. "I left that part out." But of course he had stopped on purpose, because elephants never forget. "I meant to add that the birds are really saying 'It's a catastrophe'. But there's generally not enough time for the 'astrophe' bit, and they only get as far as saying 'It's a cat'. So now you know."

Both the Big Cats thought about this for a very long time. They were glad to know how the cats got their name, but the story made them less happy about being called Big Cats. If *they* were doing the jumping the birds wouldn't even have time to say "It's", let alone "It's a cat". It was true that they *were* big cats, just as leopards and cheetahs were not – quite – so big cats, but because they were such enorrrrmous cats the name didn't really fit. In fact they were the two biggest cats in the world, by far. Yes, they did have whiskers, and they did like jumping on other animals, and they had claws that went in and out,

and they were very good at slinking along the ground; but these two enorrrrmous cats, the biggest in the world, thought they were somehow different from the ordinary, run-of-the-mill, normal, routine, regular, customary kind of cat.

"When you think of a cat," they said, "you think of something walking about a house. Or not walking about a house, but just sleeping in it. Or not even sleeping in it, but climbing about on the rooftops and making an awful noise. So if that's what cats do, we're not cats. And we don't sit on people's laps, mainly because the laps aren't enorrrrmous enough for us. And the sofas and chairs aren't enorrrrmous enough. And we could hardly get through ordinary doors, let alone those silly little cat doors. As for food, we certainly wouldn't be happy with just a tin or two of mush, which is what ordinary cats seem to like. Even if you gave us a barrel or two, it would still be mush, and mushy mush at that. No," they said, "we are different from cats and there's an end to it."

And that was how, long, long ago, these two animals, the biggest cats of all, knew they had to have a proper name each. It wasn't right being called big cats. It wasn't right being called cats of any kind, whether Enorrrrmous or Truly Colossssal or Absolutely Gigannnntic.

Now the first of these animals lived mainly in Africa and the other lived in Asia. So they could have been called African cats and Asian cats – only of course, they didn't want to be called cats at all.

The one in Africa was light brown, a kind of earth colour. The one in Asia had blackish and yellowish stripes. But there are lots of animals that are earth-coloured or blackish and yellowish, and so the colours wouldn't do for names. Elephants are earth-coloured, and so are lots of antelopes. In fact it's really quite difficult to think of an animal that isn't earth-coloured. As for being blackish and yellowish, wasps and hornets and some birds are blackish and yellowish, and it would be very muddling not to know if it was an enorrrrmous cat you were talking about, or one of these.

"No, our colour isn't good enough for a name," said the two biggest cats. "So we'll have to think of something else."

And they thought and thought until they went to sleep, just like any ordinary cat – but don't let them hear you saying that. When they woke up, which is what all cats do eventually, the one who was yellowish and blackish, and lived mainly among the trees in Asia, was very cross.

"I hate not having a proper name," he snarled. And he flicked his tail and snarled some more.

"What other noise can you make?" asked the one from Africa. "Perhaps we can get a name out of that."

"Well, I can do what the little cats call a purr, except that with me it comes out differently, more of a *ffrrr* than a *prrr*."

"Neither of them sounds much like a name," said the one from Africa. "But I suppose you could be called 'ffrrr ffrrr'."

"It sounds like someone being cold, the way you say it," said the blacky, yellowy, snarly, stripy animal from Asia still without a name. "You've got too much snort in it, and not enough *fffrrrr* the way I do it."

"That's the trouble," said the one from Africa. "No one can do it like you can, and if it was your

name, and everybody was saying ffrrr at you all the time, you'd get very annoyed. Can you do other noises?"

"Well, I often do a *grrr* when I'm cross."

"A *grrr*," said the African.

"Yes," said the black and yellow stripes. "You do that much better, although I don't know why a *grrr* should be easier than a *ffrrr*."

"Well, you could be some sort of grrr," said the African. "Where do you come from?"

"You know that. I come from Asia, in particular from India," he said.

"Then you can be an Asian grrr or even an Indian grrr," said the African.

"*Grrr*," said the stripes. "I don't like either of those."

By this time the black and yellow stripes was walking up and down, getting crosser, snarling more often, and the African knew that if he didn't think of a name soon there might be a fight. So he said '*ffrrr*' hoping to make a soothing purring sound; but he said it so badly that the one from Asia got crosser and crosser, and more and more snarly. Then the African trod on the Asian's foot,

and that was just too much. The fight started
almost at once, and fur began to fly.

"Where else do you come from?" said the one
from Africa, who happened to be on top for a
moment.

"Oh, everywhere except your stupid conti-
nent," said the striped snarler when he got on top.
"I come from Siberia, and Burma, and Cambodia,
and Thailand," and then he wasn't on top any
longer.

"Siberia-grrr," said the African. "Burma-grrr, Cambodia-grrr, Thai-oops-grrr." He said the 'oops' because he had just fallen off, but the fight suddenly stopped.

"What was that last name you said?" asked the stripes, puffing heavily.

"I said 'Thai-oops-grrr', but I didn't mean to say the 'oops'."

"Thai-grrr, Thai-grrr, now that's a lovely name. I'll be a Thai-grrr from now on. Thank you, thank you."

"Oh, it's nothing," said the one from Africa. "So may I call you tiger?"

"Indeed you may," said the tiger.

The tiger looked tremendously pleased that he had a proper name at last, and wasn't just some kind of cat, however enorrrrmous, colossssal, or gigannnntic. But the more pleased he looked, the more unhappy the one from Africa looked. It was bad enough not having a name, but seeing the tiger look so happy made things seem much, much worse.

So the one from Africa went and lay down upon a rock, but the rock was too hot. Then he lay

upon a branch, but the branch was too knobbly. Next he just lay upon the grass, utterly miserable and enorrrrmously unhappy.

"If there's one thing I can rely on," said the tiger, who was being much too bouncy for his friend's liking, "it's that you'll find something to lie on."

The one from Africa snorted a sad and sleepy agreement.

"You lie on rocks, if they're not too hot," said the tiger. "And you lie on branches, if they're not too knobbly. And you'll lie on the grass if there's nothing better."

Another snort came from the dozing shape upon the ground.

"Yes," said the tiger, "I can rely on you to lie on something."

At once there was a tremendous bound from the shape that had been lying down. "Terrific," it said, "you *rely on* me to *lie on* something. So what am I but a lion?"

"Hello, lion," said the tiger.

"Hello, tiger," said the lion.

And the lion from Africa was so excited now he had a name that he rushed around, and ran a bit, and even jumped up and down. Then he remembered he wasn't supposed to behave like that. So he slowed right down, and then lay down.

"Yes, I lie on anything," he said. "I lie on rocks, I lie on branches. You can rely on me. I'm a lion."

He was very happy to have a name at last, to have a name that made him rest whenever he thought about it.

And if you ever do see lions they are either lying down or walking just a little bit and then lying down, that's when they've remembered once again about their name.

FIVE
The L.F. Ant

Have you ever thought what it's like to be an ant? Probably not, because it's very difficult putting yourself in an ant's place, when an ant isn't as tall as your shoe, or even as tall as the sole on your shoe.

You can walk or run over a whole lawn, but an ant has trouble with each blade of grass: climbing it, falling off it, and sometimes slithering down it. The ant is a *very*, *very* VERY small animal.

So what does it think when it meets a *very*, *very* VERY big animal, such as those *we* think are very big? Well, this is a story about ants and how they have given names to other animals, and about the names they have given to animals that are *very*, *very* VERY big.

Life in the ants' nest was always busy. Even the oldest ants couldn't remember a day which had not been busy. There was never time for anything that wasn't ant business, such as fetching food, storing it neatly – well, fairly neatly – looking after the eggs, looking after the youngsters, cleaning up the nest – well, trying to clean it up – and then going out once again to fetch yet more food.

Outside was just as busy as inside. All the ants hurried along their pathways as if it was about to rain, as if they couldn't wait, as if this was their very last chance to collect food, which of course it wasn't. Almost as soon as they had dropped one load inside the nest, they would be back once more, rushing along the track, still behaving as if the heavens were about to open and this was their only opportunity to collect their last ever load of food.

As a result no ant had much time for doing anything like wondering about the outside world

and who else lived there. Of course they knew they were not alone in this world, and that there were other kinds of creature quite different from them. There were those with big beaks, and others with four legs. There were those that lived in the water, and others that hopped or jumped.

The ants always thought of these animals as other sorts of ant because they did not know any other word for them. So there were hairy ants out there beyond the ants' nest and slimy ants, timid ants and noisy ants, tiny ants and ENORMOUS ants.

A lot of these other ants were very dangerous, even if they didn't mean to be. There were the very hairy ones with ant-lers, who never seemed to know where they were putting their four flat feet. If only they had proper ant-ennae and could see where they were going!

And then there were all these other ants whose lives were so different that they didn't trouble the real ants at all. These ants sometimes went to sleep – and in the day-time! Some of them even sat on eggs. They usually didn't bother to take their food back home – wherever that was – but ate it all at once. Sometimes they fought with each other, and got up to all sorts of other strange ant-ics that were not at all what proper ants should do.

But all these ant-ics didn't really worry the ants. What *did* worry them was a certain sort of ant that had a very, v-e-r-y, v--e--r--y long tongue. The owner of this tongue didn't look very fierce, or strong, or dangerous, but that tongue was

absolutely terrifying. You couldn't see it at first, but it was there all right.

It would suddenly whip out, just when you were not expecting it and then – zap, zip – it was gone again, taking you with it if you hadn't been quick enough.

This terrible tongue would even come into the nest, lashing this way and that, zapping and zipping for all it was worth. It was gone as suddenly as it had come, but always taking dozens, even hundreds of ants with it. Then there would be a moment's rest before the awful thing was back again, flicking first one way, then the other, until – zip, zap – it was off with another load of ants.

It was bad enough having ant-eaters ant-eating you up, and all sorts of beaky birds thinking you were a tasty morsel – not that they bothered to taste, it's just peck, peck, peck as fast as they could go, and that meant dead ant, dead ant, dead ant until they were full up. But somehow it was even worse to be trodden on. Then you were just one more dead ant without even giving someone else a meal.

Being trodden on seemed such a waste, but that didn't stop it happening. Animals with tiny feet could still squash an ant, and even a mouse could squash an ant if it was not looking where it was going.

Mice were bad enough, but think of what the bigger animals could do, such as cats or, bigger still, big cats or, bigger still, horses. They didn't just leave paw-marks and hoof-marks behind them. They left hundreds of dead ants. Many a poor ant heard thump t-h-u-m-p THUMP, as some terrifying set of feet came thumping towards him, and that final THUMP was the last thing he heard before he was flattened and squashed. No wonder the ants were anti-feet of all kinds, but particularly the bigger kinds of feet, and most of all those belonging to the most frightening ant of all, the *very*, *very* VERY big one.

The *very*, *very* VERY big ant always sent the busy little ants scurrying and running back home even faster than the dreaded p-ant-ing of the ant-eating ant. This big ant was so huge, and so gig-ant-ic, that no proper ant had ever seen it. No ant had ever had the courage to stay and watch.

The ground trembled so much as it came near that the poor ants were already shaking, no matter how brave they tried to be. Branches broke from the trees as it walked. It even knocked over whole trees. It was quite the biggest gi-ant of them all.

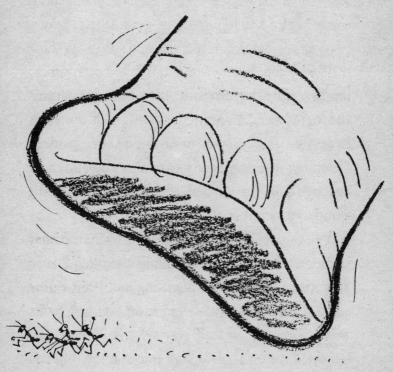

"What could it be?" they all asked each other, the first time they heard it. "It's quite the largest ant there has ever been," they said. "It's quite the largest ant there could ever be," they decided. "Nothing could be larger than this ant," they all declared. So they called it the largest ant, and wondered how it could have become so big. In the end they decided it must have grown into that tremendous size because it ate so much. "It is large because it is fat," they decided. "It has just eaten and eaten, and become larger and fatter with every mouthful." So they called it the largest, fattest ant of all, and feared it ten times as much as the terrible ant-eating ants because it trod on so many ants at a time.

In fact this ENORMOUS fat ant caused such terror among all the proper ants, when they were out busily searching for food, that the first one to hear it would scuttle home at once. As he ran towards all the others he could scarcely speak for fright. He would squeak, "Look out everyone, the large, fat ant is on its way!" but the other ants were so busy rushing around that they didn't have time to stop and listen to such a long sentence. So the ants decided they must shorten the warning and cut down 'large, fat ant' into an easier message. Then everyone would be able to stop what they were doing and rush home to safety even faster. So, if 'large fat ant' was too long, what about 'l' for 'large' and 'f' for 'fat'? "That would do the trick," they all agreed. "Let's call it the L.F. kind of ant."

And they did. Whenever one of the proper ants heard the terrible tread of this large, fat ant, he would immediately turn on all six feet, run as fast as he could, and shout: "L.F. L.F." If there was time or if he was not too short of breath, he would

cry: "Look out! L.F. coming! L.F. ant coming!
It's the dreaded L.F. ant!" And wouldn't you run
if you heard one coming your way, the *terrible*, the
frightening, the *truly colossal*, the *biggest* land
animal of all, the huge and trumpeting *L.F. Ant*?